# Escape Room

★ ★ ★ ★ ★ ★ ★ ★ ★ ★ ★ ★ ★ ★ ★ ★

## Trapped in the Snow

**AN ESCAPE ROOM THRILLER**

Written by Eva Eich · Illustrated by Marielle Enders

# STOP!!!

**B**efore you begin this adventure, you should know what you're getting yourself into… on every double page of this book you will find a new chapter in this exciting story, as well as a new clue. But this isn't an ordinary thriller that you read from one page to the next. Only by solving each of the riddles will you be able to determine which page you should turn to next to continue the story.

You will be given several possible answers, along with small details from images in the book. Only the correct answer and image will take you to the page you should read next. Find the right answer, locate the image detail in one of the larger illustrations throughout the book, then read the page behind it!

This is the only way you can escape the snowy hell and reveal the secret of the snowbound village...

Don't worry if you can't come up with the correct answer straight away. If you stay focused you won't lose the trail.

→ One example before you start:

THIS BOOK IS

① **A travel guide**

② **A telephone book**

③ **An escape thriller**

①      ②      ③

On to the adventure. Please turn these pages.

## Chapter 1

*This is the worst car ride ever*, Noah thought. The large black Audi ploughed through the slush on the rural highway, scattering several crows that had been hunting for food at the edge of the road.

It had been snowing for a few hours, and the poor visibility was making the drive even harder. He was on his way to Brockley, his hometown.

A small army of snowflakes was splattering across his windscreen, where they disintegrated on contact and were swept aside one second later by the windscreen wipers – only to be replaced immediately by countless others.

Noah ran his fingers through his dark, wavy hair before rubbing the back of his aching neck. But this didn't help lift the burden that had been weighing down on him since he received that letter.

'We regret to inform you that your father passed away in our clinic.' It was only a few words, but they changed his entire world. It had been almost a year since Noah had seen his father. The two of them hadn't found much to talk about last March when Michael Bell had visited his son in his fashionable London flat. They had strolled together through Smithfield Market checking out the traditional butcher's shop displays.

But after his father, himself a master butcher, had enthusiastically examined the pig heads and ribs, and commented on the quality of the sausages, conversation had quickly dried up. This wasn't just due to the fact that Noah was a vegetarian now.

Their two worlds were simply too far apart. They didn't share many common interests, and their sympathy for each other's problems was limited.

But now, Noah was sorry that he hadn't visited his father before Christmas, as he had promised to. If he had, his father probably would have told him about the serious heart condition he had developed, the one that required a risky operation to prolong his life.

His father had decided to take that risk without telling his son about it. *He probably wanted to spare me the worry*, Noah thought, as a mixture of grief, anger and melancholy churned in his stomach.

And now he had to go back to Brockley. Back to the memories and the empty rooms. He would meet with the solicitor to officially accept his inheritance and then drive back to London as quickly as possible.

There were now only two miles separating him from his destination. But as Noah tried to find the best track to take over the snowy road, a dark premonition washed over him. He felt certain that something was off here.

## WHERE IS THE DETAIL HIDDEN THAT CATCHES NOAH'S ATTENTION?

① **On the road**

② **In the landscape**

③ **In the car**

①     ②     ③

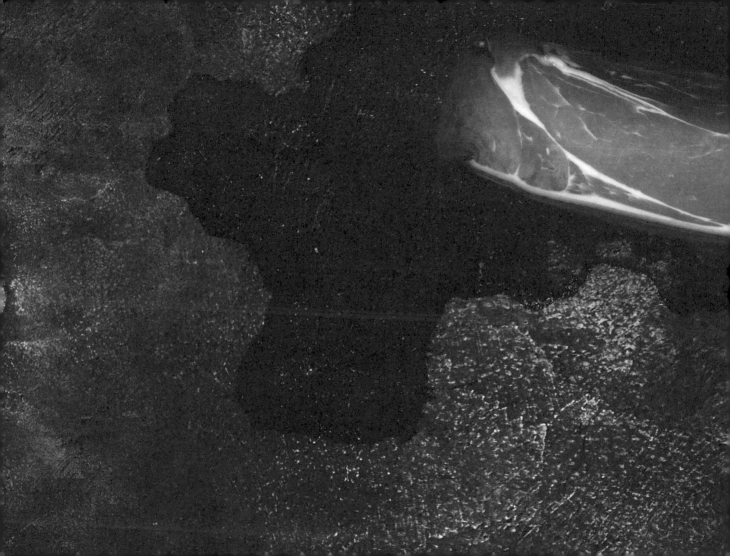

It took Noah several minutes to decipher the message: 'Things are not as they seem! If you are ready for the truth, follow the red trail.'

He swallowed. What did that mean? And who had left this note here? Was it referring to his father's death? The more he thought about this, the stranger it felt that his father had presumably died of a heart condition that Noah knew nothing about.

But Noah brushed these thoughts aside. He didn't have time for guessing games. He would meet with the solicitor, Peter Wilson, in a few minutes, quickly grab a few personal items and mementoes, and then drive back to London. He glanced at his watch: 11.55 a.m. He had to hurry if he wanted to reach his father's butcher's shop in time. The snow had held him up longer than expected, and he was making the next leg of his journey on foot.

When Noah arrived at his father's shop a few minutes later, on the stroke of the clock on the old church tower, the solicitor was nowhere to be seen. Noah glanced up at the orange lighted sign with its large letters that read 'The Whole Hog'. Underneath, in a smaller script, stood the words, 'Home of New Forest Ham since 1869'.

It was this New Forest Ham that had made the family business so successful, even internationally, for years. All sorts of delicatessens sold their ham, displaying it right next to the Serrano and Culatello varieties.

Noah's gaze shifted to the salesroom on the other side of the window. A tall man around forty years old was standing behind the counter. His dark-blond hair reached his slightly drooping shoulders and he was wearing a white butcher's apron. Noah recalled that the broad-shouldered, gangly man had been working in the shop for some years. He was also from Brockley, but as Noah had attended a boarding school in the city rather than the local school, he didn't know many of the villagers.

The salesman's face was lowered, as if he was examining something in his hand. Then he looked up, locked eyes with Noah, shoved whatever it was into his back pocket and strode out of the shop.

'Hi, you're Noah Bell, right?' he asked, extending his large hand. 'Max Chapman. I manage the shop whenever Mr Bell…,' he fell silent and his face flushed. 'My sincere condolences,' he added, gazing awkwardly at the ground.

'Thanks,' Noah said, unsure what to do next. But at that moment, a silver estate car sped around the corner. It was almost completely covered in snow. The visibility through its icy windows must have been practically nil. As the door opened, a gaunt, bespectacled man in a woollen coat jumped out, clutching a briefcase.

'Sorry I'm late!' Wilson called out from a distance. His voice had a nasal twang to it. 'I've just come from an appointment with a client in Salisbury, about thirty miles away. I took my own car, but the drive back was a little longer than normal, thanks to the weather. Well, you know how it is!'

With an apologetic smile, he walked a little uneasily toward Noah. His leather shoes hadn't been made for weather like this, and they sank into the snow after only a few steps. His handshake felt like a dead fish: limp and cold.

NOAH SEARCHED HIS EYES AS HE INTRODUCED HIMSELF. THERE WAS NO WAY THE SOLICITOR WAS TELLING HIM THE TRUTH. WHAT GAVE HIM AWAY?

① **His shoes**

② **The tyre tracks**

③ **The car**

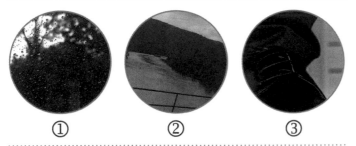

①　②　③

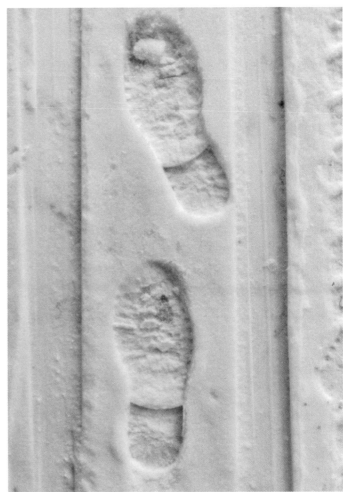

'Noah was about to lean down to follow the trail of red blood in the drainage gutter when a large shadow loomed behind him. Joseph Grimmett had walked into the slaughter room.

'How did you get in here?' Max asked as he stepped in front of the older red-haired man, whose enormous bulk was about to burst the seams of his black, quilted jacket.

'I was in the salesroom, but nobody was there, so I just kept going. I wanted to speak with you.' He stared at Noah out of small, grey eyes that almost disappeared behind bushy eyebrows. Noah knew the man. Grimmett owned the second butcher's shop in Brockley. He opened his business six years ago and had made Noah's father's life more difficult ever since. Grimmett's sausages weren't the same quality, nor did they enjoy as good a reputation as Bell's, but to make up for that, Grimmett's were cheaper. He saved money by paying his employees poorly. He didn't care how the animals – whose meat kept him in business – were treated.

'Why were you looking for me, Mr Grimmett?' Noah inquired.

'I want to make you an offer. I know you're better with numbers than your old man was. So you'll know that your family business isn't doing particularly well right now. I mean, what with the bankruptcy last year and all.' With a snide smile, he stroked his red beard.

Last April, the Bell butchery had been on the verge of a deal with a major online delicatessen merchant. But the entire first delivery to the dealer had been returned as unusable. The ham had been over-salted and inedible. Because of that, the deal fell through, and the extra ham that had already been produced had to be sold off at a lower cost. The financial loss was enormous. Unfortunately, the damage done to the reputation of the business had been even greater.

Noah knew that his father hadn't been able to get the butchery out of the red since then.

'I'll give that some thought,' Noah said, before falling silent. He wasn't the heir and owner of the company yet.

'Sure, sure. Or you could just sell me the family recipe for New Forest Ham instead, one businessman to another.' Grimmett wheedled. 'I wouldn't shortchange you.' With one final disdainful glance at Max, Grimmett left the slaughter room.

'You aren't really going to sell your father's life's work to that slimeball, are you?' Max asked. He was holding the meat cleaver so tightly that his knuckles had gone white. Noah was startled by this emotional outburst but he felt no need to justify himself.

'I'll be the one deciding that,' he replied curtly, wishing to avoid an outright lie. All he wanted to do right now was examine that drainage gutter more closely. Bending down, he realised to his disappointment that he wouldn't be able to open the grate without the right key.

Studying him, Max said coolly: 'I have no clue what you're doing down there, but if you want to open the drain, you'll need this.' He held up some kind of screwdriver. Noah took it from him without another word, inserted it into the appropriate hole, and opened the grate. Using the light on his phone, he lit up the dark cavity beneath it. Propped in the corner was another letter, as well as a small stainless steel box secured with a combination lock. Noah eagerly opened the note, which held another riddle.

## WHICH CODE IS CONCEALED HERE?

① **411**

② **052**

③ **999**

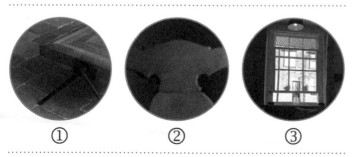

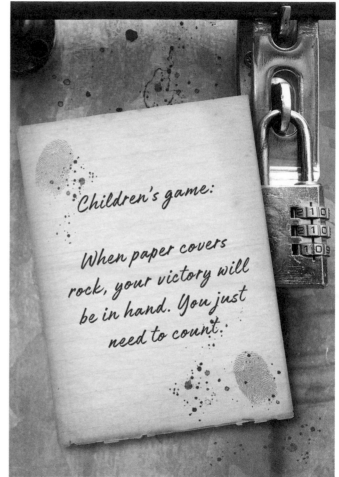

Children's game:

When paper covers rock, your victory will be in hand. You just need to count.

## Chapter 9

This time, Noah had a flash of comprehension. 'It's the numbers 7514, but each one has been connected with its reverse image!' He tried to spin the numbers into the lock, but his cold, stiff fingers were slow to obey. 'I don't have the patience for this. Someone's giving us the runaround with all these riddles,' he growled. But then his fingers started to work again, and the wooden door swung open with a soft creak. The snowy landscape cast a soft light into the blackness of the hut.

'That could be,' Max replied, 'but shouldn't we at least figure out who the joker is and why they are doing this?'

Noah sighed. The only things inside the hut were stacks of firewood and bails of hay. He cautiously stepped inside, then flinched back in surprise.

'Spiderwebs…,' he explained as he wiped the sticky threads off his face. 'No one has cleaned this place in ages.'

Max followed him, deftly ducking beneath the webs dangling from the beams. 'I wonder what surprises this shack holds for us.' He closed the door behind him and switched on an overhead light that was enclosed by a metal cage. They could see better now, although the shadows in the corners seemed darker than before. The hut smelled of hay as well as mould, and Noah wished more than ever that he were back in his spacious city flat.

At the back of the shed, an old, green cupboard stood next to a rusty lawnmower. Noah walked over and tried to open the cupboard, but the door wouldn't budge.

'Let me try,' Max said before taking several swings at the rickety lock with a piece of wood. It eventually gave way.

Noah took a sharp breath as he caught sight of what was hiding in the cupboard. Next to several other tools, a large axe was sitting on the floor of the cupboard. The steel blade was smeared with something dark, and Noah knelt down to get a better look at it.

At that moment, he heard a snapping sound. He spun around and caught Max's tense gaze. The latter held a finger up to his lips and pointed at the doorway. Noah understood: the sound had come from outside. Max slipped quietly over to the door and whipped it open. Noah heard more cracking branches, but this time they sounded frantic.

When he reached the door, Max said, 'Someone followed us here. Unfortunately all I saw was a shadow before the guy took off.'

A feeling of impending danger spread through Noah. 'Let's keep going. I'll be glad to leave this creepy shed behind us,' he said, returning to his examination of the axe. He shined the torch from his his mobile phone onto the blade and was relieved to see that the dark substance was just dried mud.

'Look over here!' Max called out. He was standing at a wooden wall that divided a small storeroom from the rest of the shed. Joining him, Noah saw that some kind of Morse code was carved into the wood. 'How are we supposed to crack the code?' Max asked, studying the series of dots and lines.

'I think I found the key to it!' Noah's muffled voice called from the storeroom. 'It's a list of symbols and corresponding letters.'

'But how are we going to compare them from different rooms?' Max asked.

Noah sighed and said, 'We'll have to work together on it.'

With Max calling out the individual Morse symbols through the wall, Noah identified them on his side and made notations with his finger on an empty, dusty shelf board. But the word he came up with didn't make any sense at first glance. Had they made a mistake?

PGGJDF

## WHERE SHOULD NOAH CONTINUE THE SEARCH?

① **In the slaughter room**

② **In the woods**

③ **In his father's office**

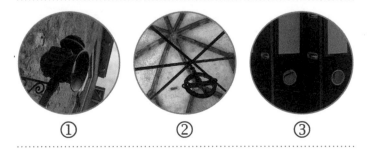

①　②　③

It was instantly clear to Noah that the solicitor had lied to him. His delay had nothing to do with a client in Salisbury. If he had just driven for thirty miles, his car would have been warm enough to melt the snow on the hood, as well as the ice on the windscreen. The only question was, what did Wilson have to hide?

Noah recalled the mysterious letter. Had the butcher's shop been doing well at the time of his father's death? There was quite a lot of money at stake here, after all. Despite making a major loss last year, the business was still worth a small fortune. Someone might be willing to kill to get their hands on it.

Noah decided to put on a good face to the solicitor. He asked the next question in the business voice that he had cultivated during his years working in marketing: 'Can we just wrap this up quickly?'

Together, they walked to the office inside the butcher's shop. Max showed them the way, though that wasn't really necessary, as Noah had spent a lot of his childhood inside this shop. It wasn't until they reached the office that Noah was finally able to shake off Max. After closing the door, he joined the solicitor at the large mahogany desk that dominated the room.

Wilson opened the conversation. 'So here's the situation: your father amended his will to stipulate that you could only inherit the business if you agreed to move back to Brockley and take over its management. The butchery cannot be sold, but has to remain in family ownership.'

Noah felt his rancour rise. Even from the grave, his father was trying to tie him to this backwater town. This revelation seemed to make the solicitor uncomfortable, too.

As he continued, he fiddled nervously with a gold money clip engraved with a dove: 'You have until Monday to dispute the will. If you do not accept the inheritance by then, another option will come into force, which I am not at liberty to share with you. Just know that it won't make you very happy.'

Noah couldn't believe his ears. 'What do you mean? It's Friday already!' he exclaimed.

But Wilson had started to pack up his papers and was about to leave the office. 'I'm really sorry, but I'm not at liberty to tell you more than that.'

Noah quietly watched the solicitor leave. He wondered if the other option Wilson had mentioned involved the shop manager. He decided to have another chat with Max and to solve the riddle in the letter. Maybe it would help him figure out what to do about the will.

He strode resolutely into the salesroom, but Max was nowhere in sight. From the adjacent slaughter room, he heard a loud chopping sound. He followed the noise and found Max cutting up pig carcasses with a hatchet. Noah froze mid stride. He had just realised what the mysterious note was telling him to do.

## WHAT SHOULD NOAH DO NEXT?

① Bend down to check something on the floor

② Climb up something

③ Cut something up

①       ②       ③

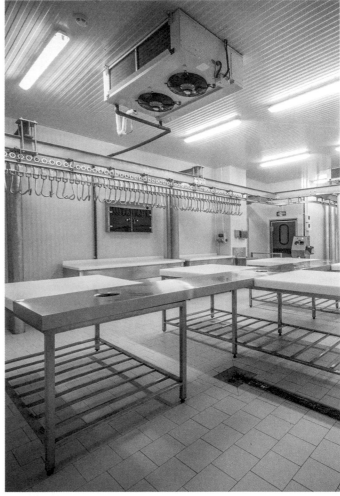

'Max slapped his forehead. 'Man, we should've just taken a picture of the line of Morse code to compare them,' he exclaimed. 'I think I'm getting old…' He shook his head. 'What do these scrambled letters mean?'

'I've seen a puzzle like this before.' Noah said. 'We have to take these letters, and see which ones precede and follow them. For example, if we pick the preceding letters first, the P becomes O, the Gs become Fs, the J becomes I, the D becomes C, and the F becomes E. That writes *office*.' Noah deciphered.

'Clever,' Max had to admit. 'So that means we need to go back to your father's office at the shop.'

They left the eerie hut and walked back down the country lane. 'I always hated that office,' Noah said into the silence, as the icy wind gushed past his ears. 'My father spent more time there than he did with my mum and me. When the cancer killed her, he spent even more time there and left me by myself in that empty house.'

'How old were you then?' Max asked, carefully.

'Sixteen, right when you aren't quite sure what to do with yourself.' Noah rubbed his fingers together inside his jacket pockets.

'I'm sorry that happened,' Max said, even though he wasn't quite sure how to respond to this unexpected revelation. 'In case it makes you feel any better, my father wasn't around when I was growing up,' he said finally. 'My mother raised me on her own, and that was on what she earned as a sales clerk in the butcher's shop. Life wasn't always a walk in the park for us either.'

'Your mother worked in a butcher's shop, too?' Noah asked.

'Yes, your grandfather hired her. She loved her job, and I think that must have rubbed off some on me. She died last year, though.'

Noah nodded. Now he understood why it was so important to Max to keep the business alive.

It took them fifteen minutes to reach their destination. By this point, it was late afternoon and the shop was closed.

Max walked around to the back entrance and pressed hard against the door, which sprang open. 'The lock's busted. It's been like that for months, but in a town like Brockley, that isn't really a problem.' Noah wasn't so sure about that – not since reading the first note.

They reached the office on the first floor. The building was silent. Noah felt like an intruder by the time they reached his father's former control centre. On top of the mahogany desk sat several folders with an expensive looking ballpoint pen beside them. A glass case nearby held the various trophies that Michael Bell had won for his ham.

'He loved this butcher's shop,' Noah said, running his hand over the smooth leather of the large desk chair. 'My father devoted his entire life to this crappy ham. I could never understand how someone could be happy stuck between dead pigs and halves of cows.'

By this point, Max had come to a stop in front of a wall hanging that featured the astrological signs. 'That's strange…' he murmured.

'Strange?' Noah asked. 'My mum gave that to my father for his birthday. I can still remember how ugly he thought it was, but he hung it up anyway to please her.'

'That's not what I meant. Look at the inscription. It doesn't fit with the rest of the picture,' Noah walked over. Max was right. They had found the next clue.

---

## WHERE DO THEY NEED TO LOOK NEXT?

---

① **On the shelf**

② **Under the rug**

③ **On the ceiling**

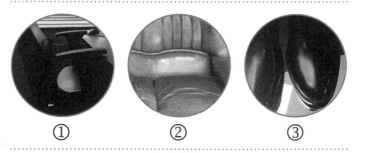

① ② ③

What isn't alive here?

## Chapter 2

How could a deciduous tree still have all of its leaves at this time of year? Then Noah recognised the old cherry laurel that someone must have planted on the country road years ago. That tree species wasn't native to the forest and it never dropped its foliage. And the leaves and the seeds in the black berries were extremely poisonous. Noah recalled that when he was around eleven years old, a neighbour's dog had died after eating several of those berries. Back then, he had happily played a part in village life, and the little stories and dramas that came with it.

Noah passed the yellow sign welcoming him to Brockley. It already had a cap of snow and the last part of the town name was obscured. Houses crowded the road to the left and right. The plaster was crumbling, and over the years, their colour had changed from white to grungy beige. The road was narrow, and Noah noticed how the old feeling of oppression was already growing inside of him.

He had left Brockley aged eighteen, glad that his business degree gave him a good reason to move away. He had wanted to be free. He had felt tired of the obligation to greet those he passed in the street and to mow the front lawn every few days. But the worst part had been his father's expectations. He simply couldn't accept that Noah didn't want to take over the butcher business.

Noah was now forty years old, tall, thin and still fairly athletic for his age. Long divorced, he had a seven-year-old daughter and was the director of a successful marketing agency. But here, against the backdrop of his past, he once again felt like a lost teenager.

He drove past the small, defunct Kino Cinema and the only real restaurant in the town. After rounding the next bend, he found himself in front of his father's house. The shutters were closed, making it look as if the windows were staring at him blindly.

Noah parked on the driveway and pulled his outrageously expensive winter coat over his shirt and sweater. As he opened his car door, he took in a deep breath of cold air.

The scent of charred wood filled his nose as dark smoke billowed out of several nearby chimneys. Noah strode down the snow-covered gravel path to the front door. His boots crunched as they broke through the mantle of snow and exploded innumerable tiny ice crystals.

He opened the large, dark, oak door with trepidation. Nothing inside the house had changed since he was last here; it looked as if his father would step out of the kitchen any minute. Even the remote control for the television was still sitting on the arm of Michael Bell's favourite leather chair.

But then Noah caught sight of something on the floor. A white envelope was sitting on the rug. He was shocked to see his name written on it in capital letters.

He picked up the letter and opened it. He skimmed through the seemingly meaningless lines of letters, and his eyes stopped on an odd semicircle located on the bottom edge of the letter.

## WHICH COLOUR PLAYS AN IMPORTANT ROLE IN THE LETTER?

① White

② Black

③ Red

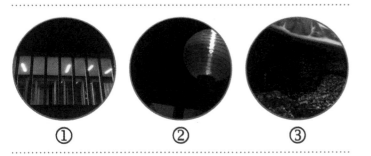

① ② ③

GTSINH RAE ONT SA YHTE ESME! FI OYU EAR DRADEY RFO HTE RTTHU, FWLOOL EHT ERD IATRL.

## Chapter 7

By the light of his mobile phone, Noah walked to the kitchen and poured a little water from a glass into the lamp. The lamp oil floated to the top and eventually reached the wick, which Noah then lit.

He gazed into the small, dim flame which brightened the darkness just a little. He returned upstairs and sat on his old bed. His bedroom walls were covered with posters from the football club he had been a fan of years ago and his bookshelf held used school books and old Batman comics. He picked up one of the comics and started to look through it absentmindedly. This had been his life, back then. With his thoughts on the past, he eventually dozed off.

When Noah woke up on Saturday morning, two surprises were waiting for him: the power was back on, and it had snowed at least three feet during the night. No cars were on the white street outside. When he opened the front door after freshening up, he noticed that the man next door was trying to shovel the snow on the pavement.

'Good morning!' Noah called, and the man lifted his arm in greeting.

'This is what I call a snowy disaster,' the neighbour remarked, relieved to take a break. He leaned on his shovel. 'The whole village is snowed in. The access roads are shut too. No cars in or out. That's why there aren't any grit spreaders out right now.'

Noah felt chilled. That meant he might be trapped here – and with a murderer. And regardless of what he discovered from the mysterious letters, the police wouldn't be able to help. The closest station was ten miles away.

He didn't just want to sit around the house. He had to do something right now, so he set off for Grimmett's butcher's shop. Something about the man with the bushy eyebrows rubbed him up the wrong way. And as he was the competition, Grimmett had a clear motive for wishing Noah's father harm.

After half an hour of forging through the deep snow, he finally arrived, nose reddened, in front of a large selection of sausages and other meats. 'May I help you?' a woman with a long, dark ponytail asked him. Her warm smile was encouraging so Noah decided to rely on his charm.

'I'd like two Vienna sausages and a little information,' he said with a grin. The woman cocked her eyebrows.

'What kind of information?' she asked as she weighed the sausages.

'About your boss. You hear things about Grimmett…'

She grinned back. 'What have you heard?'

At that moment, the door slid open, and to Noah's surprise, Max stepped in. 'What are you doing here?' Noah asked.

'I'm visiting Penny.' Max's face grew a shade pinker.

'We're friends, we discovered that we both enjoy gory thrillers so we started a book club.' Penny explained. 'To be honest, it only has two members so far.' A smile crept across Max's face.

'Well, since we're both here, you can tell me what you didn't want to write down,' Noah said. 'But not in enemy territory. Let's go ouside.' Max said goodbye to Penny and promised to call her later. The two men stepped out onto the snowy pavement.

Noah glanced around before pulling the little box out of his pocket and handing it to Max. '0, 5 and 2 for the number of fingers you spread out when you play Rock, Paper, Scissors,' Max said, turning the little wheels on the combination lock.

With a click, the lock sprang open, revealing a piece of graph paper.

---

## WHICH WORD DO THESE ARROWS FORM?

---

① **SEWING**

② **FACING**

③ **FILING**

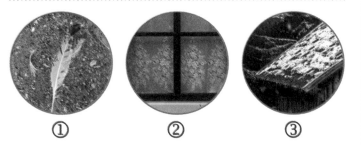

①     ②     ③

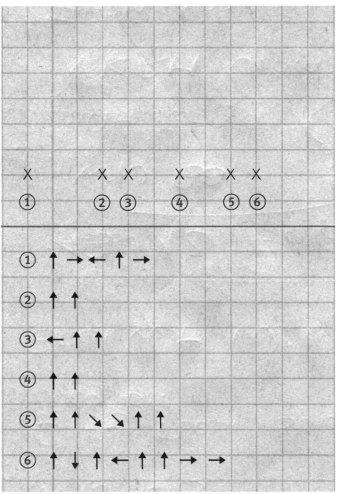

Max gazed at the key in confusion: 'I can't think of a single house in Brockley that has four different house numbers.'
He handed the key ring back to Noah. 'What if they aren't house numbers at all, but stand for letters in the alphabet?' Max asked.

'The seventh letter is G,' he counted. 'The eighteenth is R, the first one is A and the fourteenth is N, of course. The key goes to your *Gran*'s house!'

Noah's grandmother's house was located on the other end of the village, on top of a small hill. Noah would have normally driven there, but the roads were still impassable. No one wanted to risk taking their cars out in these conditions.

For better or worse, they would have to walk. Again.

Noah's grandmother had died three years ago, but because of ambiguities in her will, neither his father nor his three siblings had maintained her old home. The house was slowly rotting away without anyone taking much notice of it.

As they forged through the snow, they didn't meet a single vehicle, and Noah was reminded once again of how he was stuck in this village like a mouse in a trap. He increased his speed, and they reached the old house half an hour later, having beaten the snow.

Noah was startled to see that the beige plaster on front of the house was covered in dirt and mould, and one of the windows had been broken. He stuck the key into the lock and opened the door. Once inside, he was met by the scent of old grease and eucalyptus, which he had known forever. However, it was now underscored with a faint whiff of mildew and another sweeter note.

'Yuck,' Max said. He had discovered a half-decomposed rat on the kitchen floor.

'Come on, now,' Noah tugged on him. 'We just spent the night with a bunch of pig parts. A little death like that shouldn't bother you.'

'I have to admit you've held your own here. You might not be as much of a big-city softie as I thought you were,' Max declared, as he gave the dead rat a wide berth.

They continued on to the living room: an old sofa in green velvet, Persian rugs on the floor and a sideboard covered in the small porcelain figurines that Gran had adored. A thin layer of dust coated everything. A carved wooden cross hung on the patterned wallpaper, along with a large number of framed photographs, some of which were now yellowing. Noah recognised them, but he now studied them in more detail than usual.

One of the photos was obviously of his father, starry-eyed, trying out his new tricycle. Another picture showed Noah's aunt and uncle.

But then his eyes settled on a photo he had never seen before. It immediately caught his attention because he felt certain that this picture held the answer to all of his questions.

# WHICH PHOTOGRAPH CATCHES NOAH'S ATTENTION AND WHY?

① **A**

② **B**

③ **C**

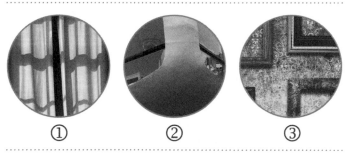

## Chapter 6

Noah stared at the riddle but couldn't make head nor tail of it. He was concentrating so hard that he didn't notice Max walk up behind him. He was gazing over his shoulder.

'That reminds me of Rock, Paper, Scissors… I played it a lot as a kid,' Max murmured.

Noah glanced up. 'Hey, haven't you ever heard of privacy?' he asked, jamming the note back in its envelope.

'Relax! You come here to the butcher's shop, pick up strange boxes and letters out of the drain, and think I'm not going to ask questions?' Max stared at him defiantly. 'And on top of that, you want to sell off your family's famous New Forest Ham recipe to Grimmett. But that recipe is this company's only chance of survival! Mr Bell never even told *me* what it was.'

'I haven't sold anything!' Noah shot back. 'But Grimmett was right that things aren't going so well. My father was a good butcher, but his bookkeeping skills weren't really up to speed. I'll need to go through all the financials tomorrow. Could you help me with any questions that come up? After all, you're the one in charge right now!'

He uttered the last sentence sarcastically, which he instantly regretted. Max seemed to be a natural butcher. It was understandable that he would want to save the business. And he probably assumed that Michael Bell had handed down the secret recipe to his son, which Noah wished had been the case.

'Sorry, I shouldn't have said that. I'm rather overwhelmed by everything right now,' Noah said, as he tightened his grip on the locked metal box.

'Of course,' Max replied curtly. They exchanged phone numbers and Noah set off for his father's house, deep in thought. The snow had now completely covered the pavement. The salting machines hadn't been through here yet. Noah occasionally sank up to his calves in the snow. He shivered in the cold wind, and when he reached the house, his trouser bottoms were caked in snow.

After starting a fire, Noah thawed out his hands and toes. Then he scoured the house for more clues, but didn't find any. He finally admitted to himself that he would be spending the weekend here – because of the will and because of the letters. With a sigh, he stretched out, fully clothed, on his old childhood bed.

He must have fallen asleep, because at around 11 p.m. he woke up to a message buzzing on his phone. Noah switched on the bedside lamp and peered at the screen. 'I know the answer to the riddle. Meet me at 1 p.m. at the butcher's shop. Max.'

The message was straightforward. Max would give him the solution in person. Noah wondered what his father's manager was prepared to do to keep the butchery alive. Could he have had something to do with his father's death?

At that moment, the lamp next to his bed flickered before everything went dark. A power outage. It wasn't surprising considering the weather. A snow-heavy branch somewhere must have landed on an electrical pole. Noah used his phone to light up the room. He needed to find a candle or a torch soon as his phone was on low battery. He remembered the old petroleum lamp in his father's room. But when he found it, he realised that the wick was too short to reach the oil in the bottom of the lamp.

## WHAT CAN NOAH DO TO LIGHT THE LAMP AND WHAT ITEM WILL HELP HIM?

① **A glass of water**

② **Matches**

③ **Scissors**

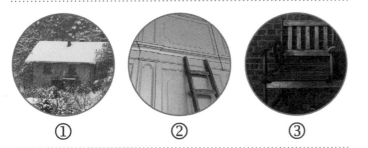

## Chapter 18

Noah picked up the box and flipped it over so that the row of numbers was upside down.

A completely different string of numbers now existed. Instead of *16 06 68 88 XX 98*, they now had *86 XX 88 89 90 91*. Just like that, it was obvious that the code they were searching for was 87.

As he turned the lock wheels to the correct numbers, Noah sensed that he was finally close to answering all of these riddles.

Max sat down beside him on an old mattress and waited expectantly.

The only item inside the box was a long, handwritten letter. Noah instantly recognised the handwriting as his father's.

He began to read out loud.

---

DO YOU KNOW WHAT NOAH'S FATHER MEANS? YOU CAN FIND THE SOLUTION ON ONE OF THE REMAINING DOUBLE PAGES.

---

Dear Noah, Dear Max,

If you are holding this letter, two things have happened.

Number one: my heart surgery didn't go the way I hoped it would.

And number two: the two of you are just as clever as I always knew you were.

I assume that the photo at Grandma's house made you suspicious about something that I would like to now confirm: yes, the two of you are brothers. Half-brothers.

I am so unbelievably sorry that I was never brave enough to tell you this in person. But everything was so complicated. Noah, you were only a few months old when my relationship with your mother started to unravel. Everything was different. We were both completely overwhelmed, and all we did was argue.

And then I met Maria, Max's mother, at the butcher's shop. With her, I felt carefree. I could laugh again. I fell in love with her and she with me. One evening in May, we did the unthinkable. I ended the relationship with a heavy heart, unwilling to jeopardise my family. It wasn't until much later that Maria told me that she was already pregnant at that point.

From then on, I supported her the best I could, but we both agreed that the identity of Max's father should remain a secret.

But now that both of your mothers are gone, nobody will be affected by this revelation. And I think that I owe both of you the truth.

I wanted you to get to know each other the way that I see you. Noah: strong, resolute and smart. And Max: a man of action with talent, passion for the job and a heart in the right place.

This is why I sent the two of you on this journey of riddles, so you would learn to rely on each other. It is up to you to decide which of you will inherit the butchery and lead the company into the future.

Just consider one thing, and this is my last riddle for you:

What do the poor have in abundance that the rich lack? When you eat it, you die. And it is the only thing that is standing between the two of you.

Love to you both,
Dad

## Chapter 11

'What isn't alive here?' Max read out loud.

'Strange question in a place where everything revolves around dead animals,' Noah murmured.

'Hey, take a look at the astrological signs. All of them are animals except for Virgo, Aquarius and Sagittarius. And the only sign that has an inanimate object is Libra,' Max reasoned, pointing at the symbol of a scale on the wall hanging.

Noah glanced around the room. Perched on top of a small bookshelf stood an old brass scale that his father had always liked. As a child, Noah had wished he could play with it, but hadn't been allowed to.

Now there was no one around to prevent him from picking up the small weights. As he cradled the little metal cylinders in his hand, he said: 'My father always wanted me to follow in his footsteps. He couldn't understand why I wanted to pursue a different profession or even go to college. When I told him that I had enrolled in business school, he agreed but wasn't happy about it. Once the dust settled, he was probably glad that I didn't want to study something like medicine. He could at least hold out hope that with my business degree I might someday take over his business.'

He broke off from his train of thought as his fingers brushed against something on the bottom of one of the scale pans.

'There's something taped down here,' he said as he flipped the pan upside down. It was a piece of paper, neatly folded and taped in place.

'I would really like to know who left all these crazy riddles and why,' Max declared, as Noah tried to remove the paper without tearing it.

At that moment, something began to buzz rhythmically, and Max pulled his phone out of his pocket. When he realised who was calling, he strode out of the room, closing the door behind him. Curious about what was going on, Noah crept over to the door and tried to hear what was being said. All he could make out was: 'I had wondered that too… thanks for calling,' and then, 'I'll do that.'

Just moments before Max opened the door, Noah rushed back over to the scale and acted like he was concentrating hard on the piece of paper. With one last tug, he removed the tape as he asked nonchalantly, 'Any news?'

'That was Penny. She wanted to let us know that she saw Grimmett follow us when we left his shop to head over to the filing shed. Now I know whose shadow I saw disappear into the woods.'

Noah wasn't sure if he could trust Max, but he didn't really have much choice in the matter. He unfolded the new note and stared at the strange images printed on it.

## WHAT DO NOAH AND MAX NEED TO GET NOW?

① Skis | ② Jackets | ③ Flashlights

①    ②    ③

1) **Jellyfish = SH**

2) **Book pages = ME**

3) **Mushroom = CO**

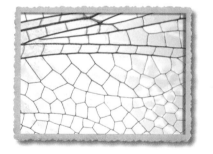

1) **Glass = DI**

2) **Barbed wire = AC**

3) **Wing = OL**

1) **Flower = ER4**

2) **Feathers = K2**

3) **Coral = CAL3**

## Chapter 14

With a little patience, they figured out the right cable to cut. The humming air conditioning unit fell silent, and Noah felt a wave of relief. He was tired of the cold.

For the next four hours, they sat on two upside-down plastic buckets they had found under the sink and chatted. Some time after 2 a.m., they reluctantly stretched out on the metal butchering table, which was at least a little more comfortable than the blood-splattered floor. The tabletop was fairly narrow, and they both tried their best to ignore the slightly embarrassing situation. They eventually fell asleep next to each other, and Noah was aware that deep down inside, he was glad that Max had stuck by his side and that he wasn't spending the night locked in the cooler alone.

Shortly after 8 a.m. on Sunday morning, Noah woke up to a scraping sound. Someone was using the metal lever to open the door from the outside. He glanced over to where Max had been, and discovered that he was already waiting impatiently at the door.

'Eddie!' Max shouted. 'I've never been so glad to see you!' He hugged the old man, who didn't seem to quite know what had just happened. Eddie was holding a large wooden wedge that had apparently been used to block the door.

'Come on, Noah, let's take the ice upstairs. There's hot water up there, so we should be able to melt it quicker!' Noah didn't need to be told twice. With stiff limbs, he swung himself off the table and picked up the heavy block that didn't seem to have grown much smaller during the night.

When they reached the slaughter room, they deposited the ice in the sink and ran the hot water over it. It didn't take long before the chunk started to shrink. But then they heard a loud knocking sound. Noah walked to the salesroom and saw a stout man in a black, quilted jacket. Grimmett was pounding on the window, and when he caught sight of Noah, he motioned for him to unlock the door. Noah strode over to the sliding door, which opened on its own.

'I thought I might find you over here. I wanted to give you a few more details about my offer from yesterday.' He reached into his jacket pocket and pulled out a bundle of money that was held together by a golden clip engraved with a dove.

'£20,000 in cash. Nobody would ever need to know about it. All you have to do is hand over the recipe.' He leaned forward and continued in a conspiratorial tone. 'You don't really care what happens to this place, do you?'

Noah tried to conceal his annoyance. Did Grimmett know what was in the will? And if so, what did that mean? Had he locked them in the cooler last night to rob him of time? And did he have Noah's father on his conscience?

'The recipe isn't for sale,' he declared. Grimmett's eyes narrowed into slits. 'You're making a huge mistake,' he replied, threateningly.

'If you would be so kind…,' Noah motioned to the exit.

Grimmett left and Noah returned to the slaughter room to find an impatient Max waiting for him. The ice block had melted to the size of an egg, and the butcher was holding a small key with an address fob.

WHO OWNED THE HOUSE TO WHICH THE KEY
BELONGS?

① Noah's father

② Grimmett's father

③ Noah's grandmother

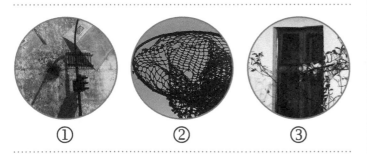

① ② ③

HOUSE NUMBER
7 18 1 14

'When you put them together, you get cooler 4!' Max called out after he identified the pictures. 'We should take our jackets along. It's almost as cold down there as it is in the snowy hell outside,' he advised as he stuck his down jacket under his arm.

They walked down the staircase to the cellar, which was so cold that Noah was glad he had listened to Max's advice about the jacket. The floor was covered in brown tiles, and the neon bulbs cast a jittery light onto the surreal setting. It was deadly silent down here, and Noah felt as if he were being led to the slaughtering block. After passing three stainless steel doors, Max lifted a large lever to open the last door in the corridor.

White tiles covered the walls up to the ceiling. The centre of the room was dominated by a large stainless steel table, and in a corner, a sausage cutter stood next to a large refrigerator. Several pig halves were hanging from a metal bar. One of the pigs was still intact, and its dead eyes were staring at the grey concrete floor.

'Cosy,' Noah declared as his breath formed a small cloud. Max closed the door behind them to keep the cold air from escaping and started to look around. Noah also began to examine the halved pigs more closely.

'So, what exactly is going on between you and Penny?' he asked Max.

'She already told you. We're friends,' Max replied defensively.

'Yeah, right,' Noah exclaimed. 'I saw the way you looked at her. And she seems really great.'

'Keep your hands off! You don't know anything about her,' Max warned. 'She's a really good butcher, and that bastard Grimmett is totally exploiting her. I've waited so long for a spot to come free over here so she could quit her job. But Mr Bell said that there'd be layoffs in the near future, not new hires.'

'Don't worry about Penny,' Noah said as he tried to rub warmth into his hands. 'I have a seven-year-old daughter and an ex-wife in London. That's enough for me.' Noah moved toward the exit.

'I'm going to get my cap, I left it upstairs. It looks like we might be down here for a while.' But when he tried to open the door, it wouldn't move even an inch.

'Let me try!' Max said, but he didn't have any success either. 'Somebody must have blocked the door from the other side. We're trapped in here,' he exclaimed as he threw all his weight against the obstacle. The door held strong as Max bounced off it and landed on the floor. As Noah held out a hand to help him up, Max glanced at the ceiling.

Against the white background in one of the corners, a message had been scrawled in red letters.

WHAT DO THEY NEED TO DO NEXT?

① **Open something**

② **Climb something**

③ **Remove something**

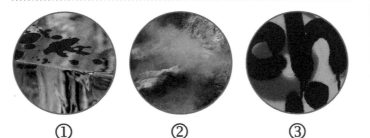

①      ②      ③

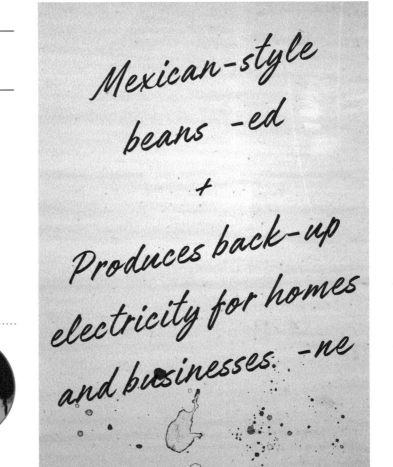

Mexican-style beans -ed

+

Produces back-up electricity for homes and businesses. -ne

'Noah pulled a red pen bearing the logo of his marketing agency out of his inner coat pocket and followed the instructions printed on the piece of paper. 'One block up, one to the right, back one block to the left, one more block up and then to the right. It's an F!' Noah exclaimed excitedly. The word FILING gradually emerged on the paper. 'Now what?' He looked at Max. 'Should I go to the closest hardware store? Or am I supposed to trim my fingernails?'

Max didn't say anything for a moment, but then something seemed to click. 'I think I know what it means,' he said, looking steadily at Noah. 'But I want to come along. You seem to have a hard time making progress without me as it is.' A mischievous grin crept across his broad face.

Noah considered this. Even if he wasn't sure if he could trust Max, they at least had two common goals: to solve the riddles and to get their hands on the family recipe.

'Fine,' he said, shoving the note and his hands deep into his coat pockets to warm them up.

'It has to mean the filing shed! It's on the edge of the woods, and since the death of the old knife sharpener, no one's used it. He didn't have any kids and the town doesn't have the money to maintain it.'

'Alright! You know the way,' Noah said, gesturing for Max to lead on.

The two men set off on foot without another word. Noah's expensive winter coat protected him from the cold, but his dark-blue chinos were anything but suitable for the outdoors. He glanced over at Max. He was wearing a thick khaki down jacket, and unlike Noah, he wore sturdy winter boots. With his pom-pom cap and gangly walk, he reminded Noah a little of his father. Although they had rarely gone walking together in the snow.

Max noticed Noah's eyes on him. 'I know you would've preferred to go on your own,' he said grimly 'thinking you don't have much use for us bumpkins. A fancy car and clever talk might help you in London, but it's different out here.'

Noah considered this, but then decided to not respond. Instead he asked, 'So you know Penny well?' When Max didn't reply, Noah changed tactic. 'What did she tell you about Grimmett? Do you know how his business is doing?'

'That big shot has his own problems.' Max took a hard kick at a clump of ice. 'He won't think twice about exploiting his workers or pulling the wool over his partners' eyes. But Penny told me that a complaint has been filed against him and that he's pretty deep in debt. That's why he'll stop at nothing to get his hands on the New Forest Ham recipe. He wants to replicate it using cheap meat and make a fortune.'

*Interesting*, Noah thought, as they finally reached the edge of the wood. A dark silhouette rose up against the bright white skeletons of the bare trees. Weathered boards seemed to creak under the weight of the snow-laden roof. 'Locked,' Noah determined, rattling the door.

He then noticed that something was engraved on the lock. Some kind of code. 'Not another riddle!' he groaned.

WHAT IS THE CODE?

① 7514

② 8653

③ 3217

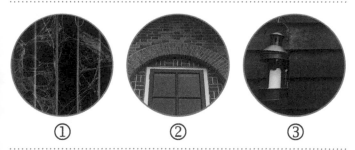

① ② ③

In the mirror, you see everything double.

## Chapter 13

'It's like a Rebus puzzle without pictures,' Noah murmured. 'Refried beans are what you get at Mexican restaurants, and when you take off the *-ed*, you get *refri*.'

'And a generator produces power if you lose it,' Max continued. 'Without the *-ne-* in the middle, you get *gerator*. When you put those syllables together, you get... *refrigerator*!'

Noah and Max uttered the word at the same moment, which made them grin despite their imprisonment.

'To be honest, we don't have anything better to do right now,' Max declared. 'Our phones don't have any signal down here, so we can't call for help. But early tomorrow, old Eddie will be here. He comes on Sundays to make sure everything's okay. We'll have to muddle through until then. So we have plenty of time to focus on the refrigerator.'

They walked over to the silver appliance and opened it. It was empty except for a large, squarish block of ice. Something had been frozen inside it. They pulled it out and set it on the floor.

'It'll take a long time for the ice to melt at this temperature,' Noah remarked as he ran his hands over the block's sides.

'We might need to put some muscle into it,' Max said. He had picked up a meat saw and was now trying to chip off some of the ice. But before he could make much headway, the saw slipped and sliced his hand a little. A few drops of blood dripped onto the ice, and Max swore loudly.

'Are you alright?' Noah asked, as he held out a towel he had found next to a sink.

'It's not too bad,' Max replied as he pressed the cloth against his wound to staunch the bleeding. 'Maybe I should reconsider this whole butchery thing. Stuff like this happens to me all the time.' He pointed at his other hand, and Noah saw several scars that he hadn't noticed before. They had probably also been produced by careering meat cleavers.

'It started early,' Max explained. 'I fell down the stairs when I was three and knocked out my two front teeth. Cute photos of me as a kid are few and far between, let me tell you.'

Noah had to laugh. 'Tell me about it! I look like a girl in all of my pictures because my mother refused to cut my hair. "But just look at your nice curls," she'd say. I secretly think she just wanted to have a girl.'

It was now Max's turn to chuckle. 'Well, you seem to have turned out alright,' he said, patting Noah on the shoulder.

'I suggest that we postpone everything with the ice block and try to improve our situation here. I'm really tired of having frozen feet. If we end up spending the night in this ice box, we can count on getting a lung infection in about two weeks,' Noah said as he walked over to the thermostat, which was mounted close to a large metal box hanging from the ceiling. 'If this indicator controls the temperature in here, maybe we can knock it out.'

Max pulled a screwdriver out of a drawer and removed the cover from the thermostat. Inside of it, they found a complicated electrical circuit.

## WHICH CABLE DO THEY NEED TO CUT IN ORDER TO SWITCH OFF THE POWER TO THE COOLING SYSTEM?

① | ② | ③

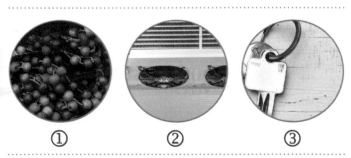

① ② ③

① ② ③

**Cooling**   **Refrigerator**   **Light**

## Chapter 16

Noah couldn't take his eyes off the photo. He was certain that it hadn't hung here in the past. He recognised himself, but couldn't recall when this picture had been taken. He must have been around three years old. Regardless, he thought he knew the identity of the other boy, who was about the same age as him, standing in front of his father too.

Max noticed Noah's concentration and asked, 'Did you find something?'

When Noah remained silent, Max stepped closer to take a look at the old photo. 'That's me!' he cried. 'You can see my broken teeth.' He chuckled, then broke off abruptly. 'Wait a second! Is that you with the curls?'

Noah nodded and unhooked the picture from the wall. 'We've obviously known each other for a lot longer than we thought… but what does this mean?' A suspicion was slowly dawning on him, one he wasn't ready to express yet.

Instead he said: 'Did you know that Grimmett stopped by the shop earlier? He wanted me to sell him the recipe and offered me £20,000 in cash on the spot.'

'The greedy bastard!' Max exclaimed. 'I hope you didn't tell him anything!'

'Of course not. I couldn't anyway since my father never trusted me with the family recipe.' Max stared. He hadn't expected that.

'For real? Well then you'll have to shut down the shop like Grimmett plans to do anyway. Without our famous ham, we'll never recover.'

Noah sighed. 'That won't happen either. I won't inherit the business unless I agree to move back to Brockley and manage it myself. My father insisted that the shop remains in the family. But that isn't an option for me. I would make a horrible butcher, and my daughter lives in London. I wouldn't live apart from her for all the money in the world. You're more qualified for the job anyway.'

'Me? Then the company might as well just file for bankruptcy. I have no head for numbers, and the debts from last year will soon force us to make drastic cutbacks. Do you think that Grimmett knows that you won't be inheriting the business?' Max asked. 'It would be a real treat for him to watch our company die even if he had acquired the secret recipe.'

Then Noah had a flash of insight: 'I suspect that Grimmett knows more than he admits, and I know how! When I met with the solicitor, he spent the whole time playing with a money clip that matched the one Grimmett had on the bills he wanted to give me. And then there was the solicitor's excuse for why he was running late. I bet Peter Wilson had a meeting with Grimmett right before he met me. He probably sold him the confidential information from the will.'

Noah had held the photograph through the conversation. He now flipped the frame over and noticed that another note had been taped to the back of the picture.

## WHERE WILL THEIR SEARCH TAKE THEM NEXT?

1. **The first-floor bathroom**
2. **The attic playroom**
3. **The basement storage room**

① ② ③

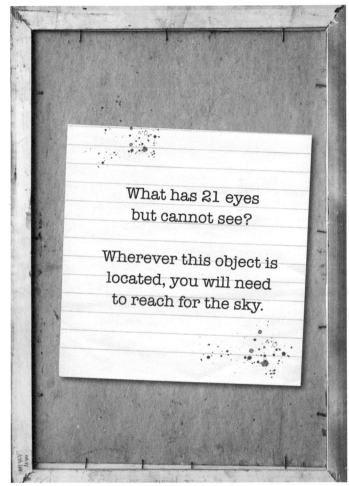

What has 21 eyes
but cannot see?

Wherever this object is
located, you will need
to reach for the sky.

## Chapter 20

'The K is in the O,' Max repeated. 'K in O, *KinO*! We have to go to the Kino Cinema, the little one in town they shut down ages ago!'

They scrambled down the ladder and the staircase as fast as they could, and then set off. As they strode through the empty, snow-covered streets, Max's phone buzzed again.

'Where have you been all this time?' Penny asked excitedly on the other end of the line. 'I must have sent you a hundred texts!'

'I was working with Noah on some riddles. Long story. I'll tell you about it later. What's so urgent?'

'Last night, I went back to the butcher's shop and poked around Grimmett's office. I found some documents that prove that he was the one responsible for the over-salted ham shipment last year. He tampered with the tanks that brined the meat.' Penny's voice sounded insistent. 'Who knows what else he's capable of!'

'He probably wouldn't stop at locking us in a cooler even though we could have gotten seriously sick,' Max replied darkly. 'We're on our way to the old cinema. Can you meet us there? Bring the documents with you, and then we can discuss what we should do next.' He hung up and quickly filled Noah in on what Penny had discovered.

'We have to go to the police and file charges,' Noah said. 'But at the moment, we can't get out, and they can't get here. We'll have to keep him in check until the roads are clear again.'

By the time they reached the old cinema, it was dark. The doors were locked, but one of the windows was broken, so they were able to get in anyway. Once inside, the faded grandeur of an earlier age engulfed them. Mirrored columns in the foyer, white display boards with black sliding letters that some prankster had rearranged to read 'F**k Brockley'. Behind the ticket counter hung an old advertising poster that featured a small talking pig with a text bubble: 'My ham is the best! The Whole Hog looks forward to your next visit!'

'That must be it!' Noah shouted. He strode over to the poster, ripped it off the wall, and found another letter. He unfolded it, and when he realised what it was, a weight lifted off his shoulders. It was his father's legacy – the family recipe for the New Forest Ham. Max and Noah hugged each other, relieved that this last secret had been revealed to them.

Together they walked out onto the street, where Penny was already waiting. Max exuberantly took her in his arms and twirled her through the snow. 'Hey, what's gotten into you?' she asked with feigned indignation, but she didn't push him away.

At that moment, they heard the sound of an engine. They glanced around and caught sight of the flashing emergency lights on an approaching police car. Noah dashed out into the street to stop the vehicle. The officer rolled down his window, and Noah asked: 'Are the roads clear now?'

'Yes,' the officer replied. 'That's why we're here. We wanted to see if the blizzard had caused any damage.'

'Not that we know of,' Noah replied. 'But we have something else for you, several interesting documents.' Penny held out a large, brown envelope to the policeman as Max also approached the car.

'Do you know where Mr Joseph Grimmett lives? You might want to pay him a little visit.' And then they began to tell the policeman the whole crazy story.

# Brockley Journal

## Taking Ham All the Way to the Top

Brockley's own Whole Hog Butcher's Shop has once again won the prize for the best New Forest Ham. Since last year, the family business has faced heavy financial pressure. But the new management seems to be turning things around.

Along with his half-brother Max Chapman, Noah Bell, son of the former, now deceased, owner, has brought the butcher's shop back to its pole position amongst ham producers. For the past few months, the famous local ham has been sold through several major online merchants. According to Mr Bell, the company can hardly keep up with the demand for its products.

The new master butcher Penny Spire is part of the remedy. She recently joined the team and is the fiancée of the second business partner, Max Chapman. Reliable sources have informed us that a wedding will be taking place later this year.

## Charges Filed Against Butcher

The well-known Brockley businessman Joseph Grimmett has spent the past week in court. He has been charged with criminal damage, fraud and assault. The case also includes a bribery charge – a solicitor is on the defendants' bench for a change. Mr Peter Wilson allegedly passed on confidential information to the businessman in question.

The court will be in session until tomorrow afternoon.

## Chapter 17

'I know this riddle,' Max grinned. 'It was used in a thriller I borrowed from Penny.'

'Then spit it out!' Noah urged.

'It's a die! It has 21 dots – or eyes – if you count up all the sides! But I don't know where we could find one of those aorund here.' Max shrugged.

'That's because it's MY grandma's house,' Noah said, practically choking on the sentence as he said it. He cleared his throat and added: 'It has to mean the playroom up in the attic. My grandma added it to the house so that we grandkids had our own space whenever we came to visit.'

They climbed the carpeted stairs to the first floor and came to a stop underneath a pull-down ladder. Noah opened it with a long wooden pole. Once the ladder was extended, they climbed up to the attic.

They were met by dry, stuffy air. Old mattresses were scattered across the floor, and a pile of board games stood beside them.

'Here are all the dice,' Noah said as he lifted the lid off an old game of Monopoly.

As he searched for a clue among the rest of the games, he asked cautiously, 'What was your relationship like with my father?'

'I liked him,' Max said. 'He was a good boss and an even better butcher. I learned so much from him.' Max broke off for a second. 'You should know that it wasn't easy for me to get an apprenticeship. I didn't really take school all that seriously, and my mother struggled to just keep a roof over our heads, so she didn't have much time to devote to my homework. I can still remember how on my first day your dad taught me that I needed to use sawdust in the smoking process. I had simply stuck spruce wood in the smoking chamber. He took me aside and said, "Max, I'll turn you into a butcher, a really good one." That motivated me like crazy.'

Noah nodded. He could easily imagine that his father had been a good teacher, as long as the subject matter had been tied to his passion.

'There's nothing here among the games,' he said, before walking over to the small chest of drawers standing against the wall. Next to it, he caught sight of a faded section on the rug. It looked like someone must have moved the furniture away from its old spot. He moved the chest of drawers aside and discovered a wooden door hidden underneath the rug.

He lifted it and shined the light from his phone into the darkness. He was almost afraid of what he might see there, but it was only a small wooden chest with a silver combination lock.

On the lid of the chest, they discovered a series of numbers, along with a clue.

# WHICH NUMBER WILL OPEN THE LOCK?

① 99

② 12

③ 87

① ② ③

Sometimes it helps to consider a problem from a different perspective!

16 06 68 88 XX 98

'Nothing,' Noah said, and as Max shot him a quizzical look, he continued. 'The poor have nothing in excess, and the wealthy lack nothing. If you eat nothing, you die.' Max understood: 'And there's nothing standing between the two of us either. At least in Mr Bell's mind, I mean, our father's mind. It feels so strange to say that…'

'True, it'll take me a while to get used to this as well. All of a sudden, I have a brother,' Noah said.

The two quite different men sat quietly next to each other, neither knowing what they should say next. Noah finally broke the silence.

'This is actually the best possible thing that could happen to the butchery. You can run the business here in Brockley. My…,' he smiled, '*our* father taught you everything he knew, and he considered you an excellent butcher, otherwise he wouldn't have promoted you to manager. And I'll come on board. I'll take care of the financials, the marketing, the distribution and all the other paperwork. I can do that from London.'

Max's eyes widened momentarily before they began to shine. 'And you'll come out here from time to time?' he asked with a grin. 'After all, we have quite a few years to make up for.'

Noah chuckled. But then he saw worry lines form on Max's face. 'But we still have one major problem. We don't have the recipe,' Max pointed out.

'There's no way our father will have hatched a plan as complicated as this forgetting to give us the most important piece of information.' Noah thought this was completely illogical. It didn't fit with the rest of the picture. There had to be one final clue somewhere, but where?

They examined the long letter one more time, but they couldn't figure it out.

'I think I need to come clean with you about something,' Max declared, his eyes on Noah. 'I wasn't completely upfront with you.' He rubbed his hands together nervously. 'You weren't the only one who received a letter from our father. I also got one. Unlike you though, I knew who it was from. Mr Bell told me that I had to stick close to you if I wanted the family recipe. This is why I wouldn't let you shake me off.' Max pulled a note out of his back pocket and showed it to Noah.

It looked just like the first letter Noah had received. The same paper, the same font. With another strange semicircle printed on the edge of the otherwise tidy note. Noah felt another flash of intuition. He jumped up and feverishly searched his coat pockets for his own letter. He found it and set it right beside Max's note.

'Look at that!' he exclaimed, pointing at the two symbols that formed a circle when set next to each other. A circle with the letter K inside of it.

'What on earth does that mean?' Max wondered. 'A small K and a large O.'

'There has to be some reason why the K is inside the O,' Noah said as he traced the circle with his finger.

WHERE WILL THE FINAL CLUE TAKE THEM?
IF YOU AREN'T SURE, YOU WILL FIND THE
ANSWER ON THE LAST DOUBLE PAGE.

GTSINH RAE ONT SA YHTE
ESME! FI OYU EAR DRADEY
RFO HTE RTTHU, FWLOOL
EHT ERD IATRL.

A STUDIO PRESS BOOK

This edition published in the UK in 2020 by Studio Press, an imprint of Bonnier Books UK,
The Plaza, 535 King's Road, London SW10 0SZ
Owned by Bonnier Books, Sveavägen 56, Stockholm, Sweden
www.studiopressbooks.co.uk
www.bonnierbooks.co.uk

First published in 2019 by arsEdition GmbH
© 2019, arsEdition GmbH, Munich – all rights reserved – original title:
*Escape Room – Gefangen im Schnee*, written by Eva Eich and illustrated by Marielle Enders

1 3 5 7 9 10 8 6 4 2
ISBN 978-1-78741-840-0

MIX
Paper from
responsible sources
FSC® C002795

Written by Eva Eich
Interiors designed by Marielle Enders, www.itsme-design.de
This edition translated by Rachel Hildebrandt Reynolds
This edition edited by Sophie Blackman

Cover images: Shutterstock.com / Kudryashka; JIANG HONGYAN; Alexander Schitschka; Lario Tus; NikhomTree
Vector; Bezzubenko22; monkographic; Ravindra37; Anton Violin

Interior images: Shutterstock.com / hanohiki; Alex Stemmer; sebra; mpix foto; arigato; Alexander A. Nedviga; Mehmet Cetin; DZMITRY PALUBIATKA;
traveiview; Romvy; Quang Ho; Wilm Ihlenfeld; TukkataMoji; My Sunnyday; Jelena Yukka; Jing H; Worawee Meepian; Lana Endermar; Stanna020; ratsadapong
rittinone; Tarcisio Schnaider; tsuneomp; Vlad-George; jamesteohart; Vicente Barcelo Varona; inxti; Alexandre Holand; Valentin Agapov; thanasus; Benjaminpx;
Pixel-Shot; Alessandro Pierpaoli; Wichai Prasomsri1; Sarawut Janeviriyapaiboon; holwichaikawee; Jerry Lin; LiliGraphie; Studio_3321; Krasovski Dmitri;
Darkdiamond67; Dmytro Buianskyi; Maksym Fesenko; Fortgens Photography; Shift Drive; IgorGolovniov; Xiao Zhou; Evikka; IvanovRUS; Snezana Vasiljevic; I.Dr;
united photo studio; Svetlana Lazarenka; Gelpi Rätsel-Vignetten; Marielle Enders

A CIP catalogue for this book is available from the British Library
Printed and bound in Latvia